+
Or295w

Orenstein, Denise G.
When the wind blows hard

WHEN THE WIND
BLOWS HARD

WHEN THE WIND BLOWS HARD

By Denise Gosliner Orenstein

Illustrated by Linda Strauss Edwards

Addison-Wesley

Text Copyright © 1982 by Denise Gosliner Orenstein
Illustrations Copyright © 1982 by Linda Strauss Edwards
All Rights Reserved
Addison-Wesley Publishing Company, Inc.
Reading, Massachusetts 01867
Printed in the United States of America

ABCDEFGHIJK-WZ-898765432

Library of Congress Cataloging in Publication Data

Orenstein, Denise Gosliner.
  When the wind blows hard.

    Summary: After her parents' separation and a subsequent
move to Klawock, Alaska, Shawn endures loneliness until
her friendship with Vesta and Vesta's grandfather
brings new insight into human relationships.
    [1. Divorce—Fiction.   2. Interpersonal relations—
Fiction.   3. Friendship—Fiction]   I. Edwards, Linda,
ill.   II. Title.
PZ7.6314Wh   [Fic]   81-19067
ISBN 0-201-10740-6   AACR2

for Harry

KLAWOCK

My name is Shawn and I haven't always lived in Klawock. I'm from New York City. When we first moved to this island, everybody stared at me. I thought they stared because I was the only girl from New York in all of Klawock. Or maybe they stared because my hair is red. I used to hate my hair.

My mother is a teacher. Early last summer, we moved from New York to this island in Alaska. I guess you know what an island is like, but this one is a very unusual place. It is called Prince of Wales. I don't know why. People think that Alaska is always covered with ice and snow, all over. That's ridiculous. I know, because Prince of Wales Island is in the southern part and has mountains that stay green during the winter. My mother says it stays warmer here because of a special air current from Japan. Prince of Wales Island sits in the middle of a silver-blue ocean and is kind of beautiful most of the time. My mother says I shouldn't say 'kind of' because it's not exactly good English.

The town we moved to on Prince of Wales Island is named Klawock. There are only three hundred people living in Klawock, which is not very much at all. There are more people living in some apartment houses in New York City than in all of Klawock. My mother kept saying we would have to adjust. I wasn't sure if I felt like doing any adjusting at all when I first moved to this island. Everything seemed strange to me. I guess I didn't understand very much at all.

I suppose I should tell you something about my father. It's hard to talk about him so I won't say a whole lot. My father has a curly beard and a bicycle with ten gears. He didn't move with us to Klawock. He stayed in New York City in our old apartment, where the doorman knew my name and used to call me "Miss." Just because my father didn't move to Klawock with us doesn't mean he doesn't love me. I understand that.

Before my mother and I left New York City, she was angry a lot. I knew she was angry because her face would get little and white when my father didn't eat dinner with us at night. I knew she was angry because she would yell at me even when I didn't refuse to eat raisins at breakfast. Mothers can get angry at you when they don't even want to. Sometimes it's not even your fault.

Here's what happened before we moved to Klawock. My mother called me into her bedroom. She was sitting on the edge of her bed, squishing a Kleenex in her hands. The bed was unmade. A pillow fell to the floor.

"Shawn," she said, looking down, "how would you feel about moving to a new place and going to a new school?"

"What new place?" I asked. "What new school?" I hate it when grown-ups don't tell you everything all at once.

"Well," my mother continued, "maybe it would be a good idea for you and me to live on our own for awhile."

"What about Daddy?"

"Maybe it would be a good idea for Daddy to live on his own for awhile too."

I was beginning to get the idea. It didn't take much to understand what was coming.

"Honey," my mother said, putting her arms around my waist, "Daddy and I need some time apart. We need to see if we'd be happier on our own, living apart."

Something cold got stuck at the bottom of my throat. I coughed. My mother pulled me close. She smelled like oranges and pen ink, just like always.

"Are you and Daddy getting a divorce? You are; you're getting divorced." I was beginning to feel angry.

"No, we're not getting a divorce." She began to stroke my head slowly. I felt her fingers get stuck in one of the knots in my red curls. "We're just separating for awhile to see how we feel."

"Why don't you know how you feel?" I tried to squirm out of her arms. I felt my face begin to get hot and as if my hair was getting redder. When I get upset, it always feels like my hair gets even redder than usual.

"Because feelings are complicated, honey. You can love someone very much but still find that it's hard to live together."

I didn't say anything just then. I turned my head away. Maybe there were tears on my face. The bedroom wall behind the brown desk had a small crack right down the middle. Just like always. The curtains around the windows were tied with white tassles; they had some tassles at the bottom too. Just like always. I looked at my mother. Her eyes were shiny. The small gold heart on the chain around her neck moved just a little up and down. I put both my arms around her and held my breath. I was angry and sad and scared. I didn't know if anything would ever be the same again.

My school in New York was on Eighty-Second Street, just a few blocks from our apartment. It used to be a pretty neat place, but lately things were diffcrent. There really weren't all that many kids in school that I could call good friends. My mother says I'm just going through a phase. I think everyone else must be going through a phase. A lot of the girls in my class were doing weird things like painting their fingernails and sighing over fashion magazines. I'm just too busy for stuff like that.

It was hard enough leaving my school, even if I didn't have a best friend at the moment. But living far away from my father was really scary. I just couldn't believe it when my mother told me we were moving to Alaska.

"Alaska's at the end of the earth," I said when she first told me. "Why do we have to go so far? Why can't we just move to the other side of Central Park or something?"

My mother shook her head. She was bent over an old, ragged map that was spread across the dining room table. I stood by the table. "Why?" I asked again. "What's so hot about Alaska?"

My mother turned toward me and smiled. Her face was kind of dreamy. She looked right past me as if there was something interesting behind my back. It was a little spooky.

"Shawn," she finally said, "I've always wanted to go to Alaska. When I was your age, your great-grandfather would tell me stories about when he lived there. Did you know that your great-grandfather once lived in Alaska?"

I shook my head. I had never met my great-grandfather because he died before I was born.

"Well, he was a very wise and special man, with a wonderful spirit of adventure. He was always reading about faraway places and different ways of life. One day, he told your great-grandmother that he was going to buy some land in Alaska and start a home in the wilderness."

"What did she say?" The wilderness sounded like a pretty unfriendly place to me.

"She told him that she wouldn't leave her family and friends, and if he moved to Alaska, he would have to move without her. Your great-grandmother was a very stubborn lady, just like you." My mother laughed and pinched my cheek.

"And did he? Did he go?"

"Yes, he did. But he wrote to her every day, and after two months, you know what happened?"

"What?"

"She decided to join him. She decided that making a new life and new friends was possible after all. But just as she was planning to go, she found out that she was pregnant with my mother."

"And that was my grandmother." It was strange to think about what had happened so long ago. If my great-grandmother had moved to Alaska, my mother might never have met my father, and then there wouldn't have been any divorce or separation. Then again, I might never have been born.

"So your great-grandfather came back from Alaska. But I'll never forget, Shawn, the stories he would tell me about his adventures there. Sometimes at night, when the wind would blow hard, he would hold me on his lap and pretend those sounds were calls from faraway places, from friends of long ago. I think, for the rest of his life, he dreamed about going back. But he never did. And that made him sad, sometimes."

"So why are we going?" I asked. I still didn't understand.

"I'm not really sure, honey. I suppose it has something to do with my needing to start a new and different kind of life. I want to see new places, see how other people live. I keep remembering your great-grandfather's stories. Sometimes you can learn things about yourself when you learn about others. It's not always easy, but sometimes it's good to take a risk and try something completely new."

"But what about Daddy? What about our friends here?"

My mother reached out and took both my hands in her hands. "We will always love our friends in New York, and we will always love your father. You'll visit him during the holidays. But for awhile, anyway, let's see what it's like somewhere else. Just you and me in a different, faraway place." She smoothed a wrinkle in the map on the table and kissed me quickly. I kissed her back, but a part of me didn't really feel like doing that. A part of me felt like running to my father and holding on to him and never letting go. I didn't know how I could ever find a way to say goodbye to him. If there's one thing I hate, it's saying goodbye.

So I didn't have much choice about moving here to Klawock on Prince of Wales Island. But that didn't mean I had to like it. The fact is, when we first moved here, I was quiet a lot — quiet and angry.

"Why doesn't this house have a den with books?" I asked my mother. I was walking slowly around the kitchen in our new home in Klawock. "This house doesn't have any kind of living room at all. What I can't stand is a house without a living room." I knew I was being difficult, but I just couldn't help it.

"The kitchen can be our living room," my mother said as she unpacked a carton of dumb-looking flowered dishes. "We'll put a big table right there and a comfortable chair for reading."

I turned on the faucet in the kitchen. The water was brown.

"Why is the water all funny? This water is disgusting."

"It's just that it hasn't been used for awhile," my mother answered. Her blonde hair was tied back with a rubber band, and she was wearing an old blue shirt of my father's. I wondered what he was wearing back home in New York City.

I walked through the kitchen door into a small room. It was to be my bedroom. The walls were covered with tan wallpaper, and the mattress on the narrow bed was torn slightly at the corner. There was absolutely nothing else in the room. I sat down on the bed.

"This bed is hard," I called to my mother. "What I can't stand is a hard bed. I'll never be able to sleep again."

My mother didn't answer. I figured she was about to tell me to cut out the whining. I walked back into the kitchen. She was standing in front of the window by the back door.

"Come here, Shawn," she said quietly. "Come see how beautiful it is out there."

I didn't move. I stood in the kitchen doorway. "It's not so beautiful." I was still feeling mad. "There aren't any tall buildings like there are in New York City, and this house smells funny."

"But there aren't any mountains in New York City like we have here in Klawock."

I shrugged and went slowly over to the window. It was early evening and the Klawock sky was kind of pink and kind of grey. Small houses, all different, were spread across the shore. Some were plain wood; some were painted red, and one was blue. The houses looked very old. The painted ones were all chipped and faded, and the walls sagged just a little. Somehow it looked peaceful to me. There were huge, wide green mountains stretched around everywhere. And all around was water. Not like the water at the beach with fast, pointed waves. This water was long and quiet. I took a deep breath. The Klawock water looked silver. I didn't say anything, but I could feel the water glisten.

I still missed New York City. I missed my father. I missed making him laugh. I even missed my old school. There's a lot of sky and water around Klawock, and it made me feel very short, very small. It also rained a lot. I couldn't wear my sneakers because my feet got wet and muddy. My mother bought me a pair of ugly green boots — I mean, *really* ugly! I was irritated most of the time.

There are five kinds of native people living in Alaska, and I'm definitely not one of them. A native is someone who lives in the place where he or she was born. The five kinds of natives in Alaska are Eskimo (sometimes called Inuit), Athapascan, Tsm Tsiam, Aleut, and Tlingit. The Tlingits are the native people of Klawock. You pronounce Tlingit like this: klingit. I don't know why. Almost everyone living here is a Tlingit. No one else living in Klawock has red hair. And I mean no one.

The first day I went to my Klawock school, I didn't take off my jacket at all. My jacket has a hood that can be tied real tight and covers up my hair. The teacher's name was Mrs. Kay, and her face was large and freckled like an enormous sea shell. She wore a white wool hat and was always tugging at it as if it were about to fall off her head any minute.

"Now, children," Mrs. Kay kept saying, "now, children . . ." What I can't stand is a teacher who calls you "children," so my first day at the Klawock school didn't make a good impression on me at all. "Now, children," Mrs. Kay said that first morning, "let's all get quiet and listen to the teacher. Shawn," she continued, tugging at her hat, "why don't you stand up and tell the class where you're from and how you like Klawock. Shawn's mother is the new teacher in the first grade room."

I pulled at my jacket sleeve. I didn't feel much like standing up. Mrs. Kay smiled.

"Shawn is from New York City," she said. "Who can tell us where New York City is?"

I couldn't believe it. No one in the whole class raised a hand.

"Why don't you tell us, Shawn?" Mrs. Kay smiled again. I thought she looked silly smiling all the time.

"Everyone knows where New York City is," I said quickly. "It's on the east coast. It's practically the biggest city in the world, with the most important people."

The girl in the desk next to mine raised her hand. She had short, dark hair and wore a blue sweatshirt.

"Yes, Vesta?" Mrs. Kay said.

"Why?" she asked, looking right into my face.

"Why what?" I answered, looking the other way.

"Why does New York City have the most important people?"

I didn't answer right away. To be honest, I wasn't sure if I knew the answer. I felt pretty uncomfortable.

"Because it just does," I finally said. "Because New York City is right in the middle of everything and is a famous, important place. I already told you how big it is, for goodness sake." My voice got louder.

The class was quiet for a minute, then the girl next to me raised her hand again.

"Isn't New York City 'outside?'" she asked.

"Of course it's outside," I said impatiently. My face felt hot. I was beginning to think I'd better skip a few grades in this strange Klawock school. "I really don't understand your question."

The whole class laughed. I felt the heat from my face in each strand of my hair. Everyone was looking at me. I could practically feel my hair redden.

"No, Shawn," the teacher said, laughing a little herself. "Vesta means that New York City is not in Alaska. Alaskans call everything out of the state 'outside.'" I didn't say anything. I thought that was the dumbest thing I had ever heard in my whole, entire life.

I didn't tell my mother, but there were two things about Klawock that I actually liked. One was the totem poles that stood on a circle on top of the school yard hill.

A totem pole is a tree with no branches, its bark carved with all kinds of animals and painted all different colors. Sometimes the totem poles had human faces carved on them, but in Klawock there were mostly animals carved on the back of the totems or on the very top. There was something about the totem poles that was special and just a little scary. In the early evening, on my way home from school, I'd see their long shadows against the dark hill and wonder how it would feel to stand so high and tall. I wondered who carved them and put them there so long ago.

The other thing I liked about Klawock was the special airplanes that came in almost every day. I thought the Klawock planes were neat. No regular planes could ever come into the village because there wasn't any room on the island for an airport. Prince of Wales Island is covered with mountains and trees, and there aren't any open places anywhere. All airplanes that come into Klawock have to land right on the water — actually in the water! These planes are called seaplanes because the sea is their airport. They absolutely never sink. Only four people can fit into a seaplane, and sometimes it's hard to get all their suitcases in the back.

If you sit up front with the pilot, you can get a little nervous about falling out or something.

After school, I'd walk down the hill to the docks and watch the seaplanes come into Klawock. They only landed one at a time, and only during certain parts of the day. Mr. Teller, at the Post Office, knew what time the plane would be landing each day. Usually, a plane would arrive just after school, and I would rush down the hill and look up at the Klawock sky. Soon I'd see a tiny speck get bigger and bigger; then I'd hear a noise, like a lot of cars coming closer and closer. Next the seaplane would move in a circle overhead. Then it would look like the plane was leaving, flying out toward the mountains. All of a sudden, it would be back again. And, with a sound that almost hurt, the plane would land right in the water, splashing until the engine was quiet and the plane stopped moving.

When it's really cloudy or rainy the seaplanes don't always come in. The pilots won't fly if the weather is bad. Mr. Teller told me that "outside" the planes can fly in cloudy weather because the pilots have a machine called radar that tells them where to go. Seaplanes don't have radar because they're so very small.

After the seaplane landed, Mr. Teller would walk down the hill to the docks. I'd watch him help the pilot tie the plane to a wooden dock post to hold the seaplane while the people came out. Sometimes the pilot had to fly without any passengers, and his plane would be filled with boxes and mail. When that happened, I'd get to help unload the smaller boxes onto the docks. The mist from the mountains and water would hang on my shoulders like a large, soft coat. No one would say much, but the silence wouldn't bother me at all.

One afternoon, while I stood watching a seaplane land by the dock, Mr. Teller called to me from the Post Office window.

"Shawn, can you meet the plane for me this afternoon? I've got to deliver this package to Mrs. Sam's house."

"Sure," I called back. "I'll meet the plane." I'd never met the seaplane all by myself. I hoped that the pilot wouldn't mind.

When the plane landed, I was waiting at the end of the dock. I was ready. The pilot leaned out the small seaplane window.

"Where's Mr. Teller?" he asked. I had never seen this pilot before. I noticed that he had a beard, but not a curly one like my father's.

"He's bringing a package to Mrs. Sam's house. He asked me to help you with your seaplane."

The pilot smiled. He threw me the seaplane rope, and I pulled as hard as I possibly could. The pilot jumped out onto the dock, holding another rope. We both held our ropes very tightly, until the seaplane stopped rocking back and forth. Then the pilot took both ropes and tied them to the wooden dock post.

"Good job," he said to me. "I can see you've done this before."

"Not really," I said, looking down. I felt a little proud.

"Well," the pilot continued, opening the back door of the seaplane, "you could have fooled me. Maybe you can help me with this load?" I nodded.

"What's your name, anyway?" the pilot asked.

"Shawn," I answered. "I'm from New York City."

"Well, Shawn, my name is Bob. I'm from Seattle."

"I know where that is," I said. "Seattle isn't all that far from here at all. New York City is much farther."

"Right." Bob started to unload a few boxes. "Hey, Shawn, why don't you stack these cartons over there, all together. Leave the heavy ones aside for later. I've got to deliver those big ones to the logging camp down by Thorne Bay."

Bob pulled a whole bunch of boxes out of the seaplane, and I put them on top of each other. Some of them were too heavy for me, but Bob said that was all right. He told me about his St. Bernard dog that weighed 175 pounds. I told him about my hamster back home in New York City, but I didn't know exactly how much she weighed.

"Good job," Bob said when all the boxes were out of the seaplane. "I could use you as my copilot anytime."

"Really?" I asked. "Maybe I could fly around with you to the other villages and to the logging camps. I could help with all the boxes and mail."

"Maybe you could," Bob smiled. "Right now you might be just a little young to do much flying around. But there's nothing to stop you from learning about planes. That's always a good place to start. Do you know what this plane is called?"

I nodded. "A seaplane?"

"Yes, but it's also called a Cessna. A Cessna is smaller than some of the other seaplanes. Maybe, when you get older, you can go to a special school and learn how to fly one of these Cessna seaplanes."

"Yeah," I said, getting kind of excited. "Maybe I could get a plane like yours and take it to New York City."

Bob laughed. "What would you want to go to New York City for? I think you're better off in Klawock with all the mountains and open space."

"My father is in New York City," I said. "And so are my friends. Klawock's too far from everything. Besides, it rains too much here."

"That's true," Bob nodded. "But you can't fly a seaplane in New York City. Did you ever see a Cessna like this when you were living there?"

"Guess not." I thought about it for a minute. "I guess Cessnas are pretty neat."

"They surely are." Bob reached out and tugged at my jacket sleeve. "I think you'd better stick it out here so that you can be a seaplane pilot some day. You know, seaplane pilots who fly to small villages in Alaska have a special name."

"They do?" I had never heard a special name for seaplane pilots before. "What is it?"

"Bush pilots," Bob said. "Pilots who fly to remote places in Alaska are called bush pilots."

I was listening so hard to Bob, I hadn't even noticed that Mr. Teller was standing right behind me on the dock. He picked up the bunch of boxes I had stacked all together. He sure was strong. Bob started to move some more boxes. He picked up the heavy ones I had put aside for later. I guess he was pretty strong too.

"Thanks, Shawn," Bob called to me as he followed Mr. Teller up the dock steps. "Get a little older and I'll let you fly my Cessna all the way to Point Barrow."

I laughed. I knew Bob was kidding. Point Barrow is very far away. It's at the very tip of Alaska where it's very, very cold. But still, as I watched Mr. Teller and Bob disappear up the hill, I thought about what it would be like to have a seaplane of my very own, and to bring boxes and mail to island docks all over Alaska and maybe even farther away.

Things at school stayed pretty crummy. My teacher was OK but nothing special. Most of the kids in my class didn't talk to me a whole lot. I guess I didn't talk to them a whole lot either. I still felt strange sitting at my desk in the Klawock school. Everyone sitting all around me knew each other. They could all speak the Tlingit language. All I could speak was English and pig Latin. And this Klawock class was different from any class I'd ever had in New York City. In my old school, the kids were always talking and throwing spitballs and rushing to finish whatever they were doing. Here in Klawock, everyone seemed so quiet, so still. When Mrs. Kay asked a question, no one would answer for a long while. George Sam might look down at his hands. Billy Ramos might look over at the door. Finally someone would raise a hand and answer the question in a voice that could hardly be heard. My mother explained that people from other cultures sometimes act differently. All I know is that the whole thing just about drove me crazy. Every time I spoke, it sounded as if I were shouting.

Sometimes the girl at the desk nearest mine would almost smile at me. Once she loaned me her red pen when my pencil got short. But at lunch, I always sat by myself and didn't get to trade my spam sandwich for something better.

One day the teacher gave us all a huge homework assignment. I was usually pretty good at doing my homework right.

"I want you each to pick a subject of your choice," she said, tugging at her hat like always. "Pick a subject that really interests you and write everything you know about that subject. Maybe, when you're all through, we can read a few in class."

I knew right away what my composition would be about. I would write about seaplanes and bush pilots. Maybe Bob could tell me more things about the Cessna and other seaplanes. Maybe he could explain exactly what makes them fly. Maybe I'd write the best composition in the whole Klawock school!

That afternoon I went to the Post Office to look for Mr. Teller. He was sitting behind his desk, putting letters into different boxes.

"Hello, Shawn," he said when I came in. "No seaplanes today. The fog's got us socked in."

"When do you think the fog will lift?" I asked quickly.

"Hard to tell, young lady. You know Klawock weather. It can change right away or stay the same for weeks."

"But I need to talk with Bob," I said, twisting my hair around my finger. "I need to talk to him right away."

"Well, Bob is scheduled to come in with the mail this afternoon but he'll never make it in this weather. Maybe he'll try again tomorrow. Anything I can help you with?"

"No, thanks." I rubbed my eyes and sighed. I knew Mr. Teller couldn't help the Klawock fog, but I couldn't hide my disappointment.

The next morning, I ran to the window first thing. The sky was all white. You couldn't even see the mountains or the water either. I closed my eyes and then looked again. White stuff like cotton everywhere. I hit the windowsill with my fist. I was mad.

"Eat your cereal, Shawn," my mother said at the breakfast table. "And stop hiding those raisins under your napkin. They're good for you."

I didn't look up.

"My cereal's cold," I finally said. "What I can't stand is cold cereal."

"It wasn't cold when I made it. Stop playing with your spoon. You could have eaten three bowls of cereal by now."

"I hate cereal," I said. "It's disgusting. I hate cereal, and I hate raisins. And I don't want to eat either of them ever again. Daddy never made me eat raisins."

I threw down my spoon and ran out the door with my jacket unzipped and my composition book still at home. Sometimes you can be mean to your mother when it really isn't even her fault.

All day at school, I kept looking out the window at the white fog.

"What are you staring at, Shawn?"

Mrs. Kay asked. "What's so interesting outside the window today?"

I shook my head and bent over my desk until the tip of my nose touched the cover of my dumb yellow arithmetic book.

That night I sat down at the kitchen table and took out my notebook and pen. I didn't have much choice. The paper was due the next morning. I had to start on my composition right away all by myself. The Klawock fog wasn't going anywhere and Bob couldn't bring his seaplane through the hazy, cloudy weather. It wasn't fair. Nothing seemed fair here in Klawock. But when I finally sat down to write about seaplanes, I kind of surprised myself. I knew an awful lot. In fact, the more I wrote, the smarter I felt. I wrote all about bush pilots like Bob, radar, Cessnas, and safety belts. I wrote about taking off from the water, tying ropes, and going to airplane school. When I was finished, I had to use a paperclip to hold the pages together. It was really long. It was almost six whole pages, without skipping lines.

The next day the compositions were going to be read in class. That morning, Vesta, the girl at the desk nearest to mine, said hello to me.

"What's your composition about?" she asked.

"Seaplanes," I answered. "What's yours about?"

"My grandfather." She looked down. "I go fishing with my grandfather sometimes. I bet your composition is good. I don't know much about seaplanes, but I rode in one once."

"Oh," I said, feeling a little happier. "I didn't use to know about seaplanes either. But the bush pilot, Bob, who brings the mail when the fog's not around, told me some things. I'm going to be a bush pilot like him someday. Maybe soon."

"Really?" Vesta's eyes got bigger. "How soon?"

Mrs. Kay stood up and cleared her throat. "Now, children," she said, "I've picked three compositions to be read in class."

I sat up straight. I was waiting to be called on.

"I'd like George, Tom, and Vesta to come up to my desk. Let's all be quiet and listen to their excellent work."

I couldn't believe it. My name wasn't called. I looked at Mrs. Kay. She was sorting through a bunch of papers on her desk. Maybe she made a mistake. Maybe she forgot about my paper. I squeezed my pencil real hard and looked down at my ugly boots.

"Well, Vesta," Mrs. Kay said, "come up here with the others. Why don't we start with yours first?"

I looked at Vesta. She was sitting very still at her desk.

"Don't you want to read your composition, Vesta?" Mrs. Kay asked. Vesta shook her head.

"Please, no," she said, very softly. I could hardly hear her. "My composition is just about fishing. I don't want to read it in class."

"Why not?" asked the teacher. I was beginning to feel sorry for Vesta.

"Because it's just about fishing," she repeated, even softer this time. "Let Shawn read her composition. Shawn wrote about seaplanes."

I didn't say anything. I was pretty surprised. Some of the other kids in the class started to whisper.

"Yeah," said George Sam, "let's hear the one about seaplanes. I once sat up by the pilot all the way from Ketchikan."

"Well," Mrs. Kay said, "I guess that's all right with me. Come on up here, Shawn. You've been elected."

I wasn't sure what to do just then. Vesta nudged me with her red pen. A boy behind me leaned over.

"Go on," he said.

I looked around. A lot of the kids were nodding.

"Go on, Shawn," Vesta said.

I pulled at my hair and got out of my desk chair. Everyone was staring at me, but somehow that was all right. I didn't think they were staring at me to be mean. I didn't even think they were staring at my red hair.

When I was through reading, I took a deep breath and looked. Vesta was smiling. She was leaning on her elbow, with her chin resting on her hand.

"Hey, Shawn," George Sam said, "that was pretty neat. Maybe you'll be the first girl pilot from Klawock. Maybe you'll give us free trips to Ketchikan."

"Yeah, maybe," I smiled. "Maybe I'll even give you all rides 'outside.'"

The whole class laughed. I laughed with them.

FRIENDS

Vesta had always lived on Prince of Wales Island. One day after school, she asked me to tell her about New York City.

"Is New York City really the biggest city in the world?" she asked.

"Absolutely the biggest," I said. "Or at least one of the very biggest. And I bet it's the most interesting city in the world, with the most interesting people. My father just wrote to me that he saw a famous baseball player walking down the street."

Vesta was quiet for a moment. I thought that maybe she hadn't been listening.

"I think it's the most interesting city in the whole world," I repeated.

"Why?" Vesta asked finally. "What makes it so interesting?"

"There are so many things to do — and lots of stores and movie theaters and fancy restaurants. And there are all different kinds of people. New York City has the tallest buildings, like the World Trade Center and the Empire State Building. And look at Klawock. It probably has the smallest buildings anywhere in the world."

"Oh," Vesta said. She was quiet again for a long time. I pulled on my hair for a minute. I don't know why, but I was feeling very squirmy all of a sudden.

"I suppose," Vesta finally continued slowly, "I suppose families are very big in New York City. They must be really big."

I had no idea what Vesta was talking about.

"Vesta," I said, "why do families in New York City have to be real big? I don't

have a brother or sister. I don't even have
a dog." My voice was getting louder.

"Hmmmmm," Vesta said softly. "If
you don't have big families in New York
City, then why do you have to have so
many tall buildings?"

I felt my face get warm. I felt my hair
redden. There was no question about it; I
was angry. I snatched up my school books

from my desk and zipped up my jacket.

"For goodness sake, Vesta," I kind of yelled, "you don't understand anything. No one in dumb Alaska understands anything at all."

And then I turned and ran right out of the room. I ran away from Vesta's quiet face. Sometimes I have a temper that I just can't hide. Sometimes I say things that maybe I shouldn't.

After I got out of breath from running, I walked slowly home. It was raining. The bottom of my jeans were soggy. I felt my hair curl and curl. I didn't really care.

My mother was in the kitchen when I got home. She was correcting school papers.

"Want a cup of cocoa?" she asked, hardly looking up. She wasn't angry a lot like she was in New York, but here she was always tired or busy.

"No," I said. I sat down at the table across from her. The chair squished each time I moved. I turned from side to side for awhile, listening to the squishing.

"Mom," I asked, "New York is the biggest city in the world, right?"

"Well, it's one of the top ten," she answered.

"But it's the most interesting, most important city — I mean, it's really different from other places, isn't it?"

"Oh, I don't know. Not all that much different. Bigger, perhaps, and exciting, but a lot of cities are like that. A city is a city. Why?"

I didn't say anything else just then. What I wondered was this: How could anyone be happy in this village named Klawock and not want to move to a big city like New York?

The next day at school, I kept my head down most of the morning. I didn't look at Vesta at all. During the spelling test, I wrote so hard that my pencil top broke. But just before lunch, someone tugged at my sleeve. It was Vesta. She was smiling.

"Shawn," she said, "I brought you something."

I was surprised. I had thought that Vesta might be mad at me. She and I walked out of school together, and we sat on the steps just outside the front door. For once it wasn't raining. We could look down the hill from those steps and see the docks below and the misty, green mountains. Vesta opened her paper bag and handed me something wrapped in newspaper.

"Salmon," Vesta smiled, "smoked salmon from my father. He caught it by Bristol Bay last summer. I helped in the smokehouse. This is the kind of fish we send to cities all over the country."

I had once tasted smoked salmon in New York City. My mother bought it at the delicatessen along with some rye bread. She called it lox. This stuff looked different somehow. I took a bite but nothing came off. Vesta laughed.

"Harder," she said. "Harder with your teeth; like this."

She took an end of the salmon in her teeth and pulled quickly. A small piece disappeared into her mouth. I took another bite and pulled quickly like Vesta. A big chunk of salmon fell into my lap.

"Chew," nodded Vesta, chewing pretty hard herself.

I put the chunk of salmon into my mouth. It was very hard and kind of salty. And then I began to chew.

I can tell you, chewing Vesta's smoked salmon wasn't easy. The faster I chewed, the more my mouth got tired. But the more I chewed, the better it tasted. Vesta and I sat on the school steps and chewed and chewed. Our hands smelled funny from pulling at the fish. Our faces looked dirty from the salmon grease. We didn't care. We didn't talk much, but I knew we both felt good.

"Vesta," I said after a while, "your smoked salmon is good. We have smoked salmon in New York City but it's different. Good, too, but just different."

Vesta nodded. We both wiped our faces on our shirt sleeves and went back into school together.

The next day, Vesta invited me to her house. I had never been there before. Vesta's house was small, really just one large room that went around a corner. In that corner was a kitchen with a wood-burning stove. You have to keep that stove filled with a lot of wood so that the house can stay warm and so that you can cook. The beds in Vesta's house had curtains across them. Vesta said you could pull those curtains together before you go to sleep if you want to be all alone. I liked Vesta's house. It was quiet and cozy, and it somehow felt familiar. I didn't feel strange in Vesta's house at all.

Vesta's mother was nice too. She had dark hair, just like Vesta's, but she wore it on top of her head tied with a yellow scarf. She seemed to like Vesta a whole lot. Vesta's mother smiled at me all the time. She made us a drink called Russian tea. This is what Russian tea tastes like: Christmas. It's from oranges, cinnamon, and many other spices. Vesta said that once Russian people lived in Alaska and some of them lived in Klawock. Russian tea makes your nose run, but it's worth it.

Soon, I was going to Vesta's house a lot. The thing was, Vesta's mother didn't work during the day and was always home to make tea and small cakes. Every once in a while, I would get to wishing that our house was more like Vesta's house. I even wished that I had curtains around my bed and that someone was always home when I got there.

One day, Vesta and I were drinking Russian tea at her house when a tall man came in. He was old. I knew right away that he was Vesta's grandfather. I knew that because I had heard all about him from Vesta. She thought he was really something. Vesta's grandfather was carrying a walking stick and wore a brown parka. It had a hood just like my jacket. He walked in slowly, looked at me, but didn't speak. My hair started to feel very red. Vesta and her mother began talking to him in Tlingit. I didn't understand what they were saying, so I decided to go home.

All the way home, I thought about Vesta's grandfather. There was something about him that bothered me, but I didn't know exactly what. Somehow, I had the feeling that he just didn't like me much. Somehow, I had the feeling that he didn't think I belonged in Vesta's house at all.

I guess I could have asked my mother why Vesta's grandfather didn't like me, but she would have said that it was my imagination. I guess I could have asked Vesta why her grandfather didn't like me, but that might make her feel embarrassed. I didn't want to do that. Vesta and I liked each other too much for that.

Since the time Vesta and I ate salmon on the school steps, we had gotten to be good friends. You could even call us best friends. Anyway, Vesta and I started doing all kind of things together. Like looking on the beach for starfish and shells, and old boat parts. Like helping each other with homework, and sharing each other's sandwiches, and hanging out at the docks to watch the bush pilots land their Cessna seaplanes. Just things that kids like to do. One day, we found a glass ball on the beach. Vesta said it came from a World War II Japanese fishing-boat net. I don't know how she knew that. I still keep that glass ball on the little table by my bed, and sometimes wonder how it got to this small island, all the way from Japan.

Vesta was different from any friend I'd ever had. She didn't talk as much as my friends in New York City. She didn't talk as much as I did. But she knew a whole lot about all kinds of things and was very good at teaching me. Vesta could tie three kinds of rope knots with her eyes closed, and she could hop backwards on ice without slipping. She knew how to clean fish. She could say hello in English and Russian and in Tlingit, too. Vesta would never push you to get at the head of the line or hurry to eat the extra dessert. When she wrote at her desk at school, her hand moved slowly and carefully. When she listened to you talk about feeling funny or different, she would nod her head. Sometimes I thought that Vesta had a grown-up person inside her clothes. She seemed to know how to do things, and she listened to what I knew.

One Saturday, Vesta and I decided to go berry picking.

"It'll be the last chance we get," Vesta said, pulling a big straw basket down from her kitchen shelf. "Soon, it will be too cold and all the bushes will be bare. The best berries are out by the garbage dump, way at the end of the island."

I looked at my green boots and shook my head. We had a long walk in front of us.

It was drizzling, like most Klawock days, and the mud under my feet turned my green boots dark brown. Vesta was walking quickly. I had to skip every once in a while just to keep up.

"Hurry up, Shawn," Vesta would call. "We've got to do a lot of picking before dark."

"OK, OK," I said, "but I hope these berries are worth it."

Vesta laughed.

"Oh, they are. We pick lots of good berries all summer and all fall so that we can eat them in winter. First you soak them in salt. Then you freeze them or make jam for toast.

"Salt?" I stopped walking for a minute. "Why do you soak them in salt?"

"That's to get the worms out. Sometimes berries have tiny worms inside.

52

When you soak them in salt, the worms come out."

I was beginning to think I wasn't going to like berry picking too much.

"What if you eat a worm by mistake?" I asked.

"Oh, nothing." Vesta's eyes flashed. "Grandfather says worms are full of vitamins. Come on, Shawn, hurry up. It's not too much longer now."

Vesta and I walked and walked.

"There's sure a lot of mud here," I said. "There's hardly any mud at all in New York City."

Vesta looked surprised.

"How does the earth stay dry?" she asked.

"Well, there isn't exactly earth in New York City," I said. "It's more like cement all over."

"And the cement dries out the earth?"

I looked down. Sometimes Vesta asked me things I just didn't know. Sometimes that made me feel not quite as smart as usual.

Finally the path narrowed, and then it

suddenly stopped altogether.

"We're at the garbage dump now,"
Vesta said. "Look over there — that's
where the best berry bushes are."

There were all kinds of different berries in those bushes. There were blackberries, blueberries, and salmonberries,
named after the pink salmon fish. When
you pick a lot of berries, your fingers get
sore and stained with berry juice. And
sometimes, you forget about worms and
eat a bunch of berries, no matter what.

It was kind of peaceful in the woods.
The rain had stopped completely, and the
Klawock sun kept drifting in and out be-
tween the yellow and grey clouds. I took

down my hood and shook out my curls.
My hair was getting longer. I hadn't had it
cut since the beginning of school. I looked
over at Vesta. Every once in a while, the
sun would hit her very black hair and
make it shimmer. She was humming
softly to herself and carefully picking berries as if each one was something special.
Suddenly she looked up.

"You know, Shawn," she said, rocking
her berry basket in her arms like a little
baby, "when I first started school, a long
time ago, everyone laughed."

"Who laughed?" Sometimes Vesta
had a way of talking that made you have
to ask a lot of questions.

"They did. The kids at school." Vesta looked away and started picking again. "Even the teacher did, once."

"Why in the world did they laugh? What were they laughing at?"

"They were laughing at me," Vesta said.

I stopped picking berries and turned to look at Vesta carefully. Her face looked a little pink. She brushed a strand of hair from her face.

"Why?" I asked again.

"Because of the smokehouse," Vesta said. "For a long time, my family didn't have a good house. In the winter, the roof would crack. Everything would freeze. So we had to sleep in the smokehouse. We kept warm from the burning cedar chips."

"What cedar chips? What smokehouse? Isn't a smokehouse a place where you make salmon like the kind you bring to lunch?"

Vesta nodded.

"In the smokehouse," she continued, softly, "we hang salmon strips to dry out. They hang in the smoke of burning wood chips. Cedar wood. The cedar smoke makes the salmon taste right."

"Oh," I said, beginning to understand a little. "But why did everyone laugh about the smokehouse?"

"It was the smell." Vesta was staring at one blueberry very hard. "The smoke smell. The fish smell. The smells got in my clothes and in my hair. I smelled different."

"And they all laughed at you? That's just absolutely the dumbest thing I've ever heard, and they're absolutely the biggest creeps and sure don't know anything at all! Boy!"

I was angry. I put down my basket and stuck my hands on my hips for emphasis.

"Shawn," Vesta said, almost in a whisper, "It hurt. They called me names. They pointed. I held my head all the way down."

"Oh, Vesta." I swallowed hard to get rid of the lump in my throat. "I wish I'd been around. I would have made them stop."

Vesta smiled. Her eyes were bright.

"I know," she said. "You're a strong friend."

"Yeah, I am. I would have shown them a thing or two. I would have punched out their lights."

"Lights?"

"That's just an expression," I explained. "An expression like 'outside.'"

"I see." Vesta looked confused. "But what lights?"

"Vesta!" I stamped my foot in the mud. "It's just an expression. There aren't any real lights."

Vesta shook her head and started to giggle softly. I stared at her. She looked funny, giggling into her berries. I started to laugh, too. Soon, we were both laughing so hard that there were tears in our eyes and our faces got red and our stomachs hurt. We just couldn't seem to stop laughing at all.

Finally, Vesta took a deep breath. And then another.

"Enough, Shawn," she said, still laughing just a little. "We have to get more berries before it gets dark."

Just as I was popping a fat salmon-berry into my mouth, I heard a twig or something crack behind me.

"Hey, Vesta," I called, "these salmon-berries are pretty neat. Want some of mine?"

I turned around and then suddenly stopped. There was a funny brown animal right in front of my feet. It looked like something I had seen at the Central Park Zoo. No doubt about it — a small bear was staring at me.

"Vesta," I called out, slipping a little in the mud, "I think there's something here that's not supposed to be . . ."

The bear was still staring at me. Its fur was chocolate brown. It looked soft. Its eyes were very large, with curly lashes, just like a person. I knew I shouldn't move. The bear was shaking his head from side to side. I almost wanted to touch him. He wasn't that big at all.

"Shawn," Vesta called back, "Where are you? Where's . . ."

Suddenly Vesta appeared from behind the bushes. When she saw the bear, she stopped right away. I still didn't move. The bear looked at Vesta, looked at me again, turned and trotted away. I giggled. It looked funny, wiggling its bear rump from side to side.

"Shawn," Vesta said, grabbing my hand, "we'd better get away from here. That was a baby bear, a cub. If its mother is around, we're in big trouble."

"Why?" I asked. "The bear's gone now. Let's pick some more berries."

Vesta shook her head.

"If the mother bear sees us around her cub, she'll be real mad. Mother bears are bigger than their cubs."

What Vesta said made a lot of sense. I picked up my berry basket and began to walk quickly down the narrow path toward town. Vesta walked quickly beside me. We looked at each other. We both broke into a run.

My mother was angry when we told her about the bear.

"You kids should know better," she said, helping me off with my boots. "From now on, no wandering off in the woods without an adult. Do you understand?"

I nodded. That sounded like a pretty good idea to me. Vesta nodded too.

"Maybe we'll bring Grandfather along next time," Vesta said.

"That's a good idea," my mother said.

I didn't say anything. I didn't think that was a good idea at all.

The next day after school, guess who was standing on the front steps where Vesta and I ate our lunch. It was Vesta's grandfather. He was standing there looking out toward the Klawock water, wearing his brown parka and carrying his walking stick. I felt funny. I didn't want to talk to Vesta's grandfather, but of course, Vesta ran right up to him. He nodded at her and then looked straight at my red hair.

"Hello," I said, looking down. I didn't want to be rude. Vesta liked her grandfather an awful lot. He didn't say anything but kept looking at me. I decided to put up my hood. He turned back to Vesta and held up one hand. I noticed that it was shaking. I wanted to get away very fast. Vesta's grandfather cleared his throat and then started speaking very slowly.

"Granddaughter, listen to me now. When you see the bear, do not be afraid. You must not be afraid but you must keep calm. Stay calm all the way down inside and the bear will understand."

I looked at Vesta. She was staring intently at her grandfather, almost as if in a trance. No one said anything for a minute.

"Yes, Grandfather," Vesta finally said.

The tall, old man nodded and then slowly, one step at a time, walked down the school steps.

The next time I saw Vesta's grandfather I was in John Petrovitch's store. Petrovich is a Russian name. Maybe Mr. Petrovitch is related to the Russians who used to live here. He is also the mayor of Klawock and knows everyone who lives here. He once showed me a blue tattoo on his left wrist. It's in the shape of a heart. I always like going to Mr. Petrovitch's store. It's full of all kinds of things, like crackers and camera film and flannel shirts and dried fish. Once I saw a rifle for sale there.

Vesta's grandfather was showing Mr. Petrovitch a white wolf hide. I think he had trapped it himself. I nodded to Vesta's grandfather when I came in the store and pulled up my jacket to cover my red hair.

"Hello, Shawn," Mr. Petrovitch said. "What can I do for you?"

I stared at my ugly green boots. Somehow I felt strange in front of Vesta's grandfather. Both men were looking right at me. I pulled on the strings of my jacket hood.

"Shawn?" Mr. Petrovitch said.

I knew I had to say something.

"Mr. Petrovitch," I kind of mumbled, "my mother needs some lettuce and powdered milk."

This is what I can't stand: No one in Klawock drinks regular milk from a carton. You can't have milk without cows, and there just aren't any cows in Klawock. Cows need to eat grain in order to stay healthy and give milk. There's absolutely no grain on Prince of Wales Island. Grain comes from wheat. The rocky soil and cold, damp weather here won't let wheat grow. If the people in Klawock had milk sent from "outside," the milk would go sour on the long, long trip. So everyone has to drink powdered milk. It tastes disgusting.

"Well, Shawn," Mr. Petrovitch said, "I'll be happy to sell you some milk, but the lettuce is no good. It froze on the way up from Seattle."

Sometimes the weather in Alaska is so cold that things freeze quickly. Since the Klawock soil doesn't have the right minerals for vegetables to grow in, we order lettuce and other fresh things from Seattle. When the weather is real, real cold, the fresh things from Seattle freeze before we can even eat them. It's a pretty long trip from the state of Washington, so we hardly eat fresh vegetables anymore. Most of the stuff we eat is canned because canned food almost never goes bad.

"OK, Mr. Petrovitch," I said, quickly. "I'll just take the milk."

All this time, Vesta's grandfather was quiet, but I could feel him looking at me. I couldn't shake the feeling that he didn't like me very much. All the way home, I wondered why.

The very next afternoon, when I came home from school, my mother called me into the kitchen. She was making deer stew. Sometimes people call deer meat *venison*. I don't know why.

"Shawn," she said, stirring the stew with a big wooden spoon, "I made some stew for Vesta's grandfather. The hunting season has been bad this year. Hardly any deer or bear around. Vesta's mother says that they barely have enough to last the winter. And I worry about the grandfather, all alone at the end of the island. He's getting to be an old man and could use a little looking after."

I didn't say anything. He seemed old enough to look after himself. My mother put the spoon down.

"I'd like him to have some of this stew for dinner. I think he'd really appreciate a hot meal and some company."

I looked away. I knew what was coming.

"Shawn," my mother continued, "would you please take a bowl of the stew over to Vesta's grandfather's house after school tomorrow?"

I pulled at my hair. A bunch of curls were stuck in a big knot.

"Why do I have to?" I asked.

"I just finished telling you," she said very slowly. "Vesta's grandfather is living all alone, way out at the end of the island. He's an old man and can hardly hunt and cook for himself. It seems to me that you would want to do something for your friend's grandfather."

I bit my lip.

"Well, I don't," I said.

And then I ran right out of the room. My mother followed me. I was lying on my bed with my head under the pillow. She sat down next to me and put her hand on my back. My mother has very soft hands. They feel good against your back if you just might cry.

"Honey," she said, stroking my back, "I know living here has been a big adjustment for you. It has for me, too. I know that you're trying hard."

I took the pillow off my head and looked up. There were tears on my face. My mother put her arms around me and held me for awhile.

"You know," she continued, "it's hard for everyone, making changes. Sometimes it seems as though nothing will ever be right again. But I want you to know that I'm very proud of you. You've been making a real effort. It's not easy being away from everything familiar. I guess it's lonely for us both. We need to reach out to more people here, call out to new friends. I probably need to do more of that, too, instead of burying myself under my work. But we can always count on each other, can't we? We're lucky we have each other, and I think we'll soon feel better about things, don't you?"

Sometimes I love my mother so much, my heart hurts.

When I got home the next day after school, I poured a bunch of deer stew into a bowl. I wondered whether one bowl was enough. Vesta's grandfather might eat a lot. I covered the bowl with tinfoil so it wouldn't spill while I was walking. Then I sat down and stared at the bowl of deer stew for a long while. Finally I picked it up and left.

When I knocked on the door of the house, no one answered. I knocked again, then pushed the door gently. It opened halfway.

"Hello," I said quietly. "Hello," I said again, louder.

I looked inside. Vesta's grandfather was sitting at the kitchen table, cutting a piece of wood with a knife. He didn't look up. I walked into the house and put the bowl of stew on the table for him to see.

"My mother and I thought you might like some deer stew," I said. "My mother made it herself. Some people call deer meat *venison*. I don't know why."

Vesta's grandfather reached out and touched the bowl with his fingertips. And then he looked up at me. His face looked different from any other face I had seen. His skin was the color of wood, and the lines on his face were like the grain of wood. The eyes were very dark, very large, and very still. He looked beautiful to me. Suddenly I didn't feel so scared.

"Thank you, young Shawn," he said, nodding. I was pretty surprised. He had never spoken to me before. I didn't even know he knew my name. It made me feel kind of good to know that he did.

"You're welcome," I said. "But I didn't make the stew. I just carried it over here from my house. My mother thought you might like it for your dinner. I hope it tastes good for your dinner tonight." Sometimes, when I get nervous, I start repeating myself. Vesta's grandfather made me a little nervous.

"Well," I said, "hope it tastes good for your dinner."

And then I turned around and left the house very quickly. I took the road at the bottom of the school yard hill. It was beginning to get dark, and I could barely see the totem poles way up on top of the hill. I shut my eyes and opened them again.

I thought I could see the totems moving in the hazy Klawock light; for a minute, it seemed as if they swayed and leaned towards me.

The next day at dinner I chewed my fish slowly; I drank my powdered milk slowly. Do you know what I was thinking about? I was thinking about what Vesta's grandfather was having for his dinner. That's kind of crazy because I still wasn't sure that I liked him all that much. Being around him still made me feel funny, like I looked all wrong, like my hair was getting redder. But all the same, while I was eating my dinner that night, I wondered if he was eating his dinner too.

"You're very quiet tonight, Shawn," my mother said all of a sudden. "Are you feeling all right? Have you been at my cooking chocolate again?"

I shook my head.

"I'm feeling fine."

"Well, eat all your dinner. At this rate, we're going to be at the table until it's time to go to school in the morning."

"Mom," I said, spreading my fish around my plate, "is it hard to make deer stew?"

"Not too hard. Why?"

"I dunno. Just wondering."

"Maybe next time Mr. Sam brings us some fresh meat, I'll show you how. OK?" Mr. Sam was the best hunter in the whole village. He knew how to trap animals so that they didn't suffer much.

"OK," I answered.

That night in bed, just before I fell asleep, I decided what I was going to do. Tomorrow I would make Vesta's grandfather some dinner. After all, he was important to Vesta, and Vesta was important to me. I rolled over in my bed. That was what I would do the very next afternoon. And I wasn't even going to tell Vesta.

After school, I ran home as fast as I possibly could. I knew my mother wouldn't get there until late. She had some kind of teachers' meeting. When my mother has a meeting or something after school, she leaves me a sandwich in the refrigerator. I opened the refrigerator door. There it was, a sandwich with some pink stuff inside: Spam. I did what I usually do when my mother leaves Spam around. I wrapped the sandwich in a few napkins and stuck it in the garbage. I understand that I shouldn't waste food. There are a lot of people who don't have any food at all. I understand something else too: I hate Spam.

Instead, I took some cookies from the box my mother hides behind the dishes and sat down at the kitchen table. I can eat cookies very fast. I thought about what Vesta's grandfather might like for his dinner. I took out the cookie box again and dumped a bunch of cookies into a napkin. Next, I looked in the cabinet over the sink. Perfect — a packet of Kool-Aide. What else might Vesta's grandfather want for his dinner? A big can of corn was on top of the refrigerator. I stood on a chair and pulled it down. I was finished.

When I got to his house, I knocked on the door, waited for a minute, and then walked in. Vesta's grandfather was sitting at the table, just like before. He was cutting a piece of wood with a knife. Just like before. There was no reason to be nervous.

"Hello, young Shawn," he said.

"Hello," I said, setting his dinner down on the table. "I brought you something to eat. I thought you might like some more dinner tonight. This time, I made your dinner all by myself. My mother is at a teachers' meeting tonight."

Vesta's grandfather might have smiled just a little. It was hard to tell. He put one hand on my arm and pointed to a chair.

"Sit down," he said.

I sat down next to him. He picked up the piece of wood again and began cutting it with a knife. I had seen other men in Klawock cut wood like that. It's called carving. It's a kind of artwork. Vesta's grandfather began to talk as he carved. This is what he said:

"This wood is like the pulse of a wrist. It's full of motion and warm inside the hand. What I am carving is alive."

I watched the piece of wood change shape as he carved. It looked like magic. All at once, I could see the shape of a small, curved paddle.

"Are you carving a paddle?" I asked. He nodded.

"This is a paddle like those from long ago. All we had to move our boats in those days were paddles. We had no engines. Even then, we carved our paddles like pieces of art. When I was small, like you, my uncle taught me to carve as I am carving now. My uncle was an artist and taught me not to do anything halfway. The Tlingit people treat art as something alive, something to be respected."

Vesta's grandfather had a way of speaking that really made you listen. Maybe it was because he spoke so softly. Maybe it was because he didn't speak often. Kind of like Vesta.

"Have you ever carved a totem pole?" I asked.

Vesta's grandfather nodded. "The totem pole in Klawock with the red fox on top, I carved that."

I couldn't believe it. The fox totem pole was my favorite. He continued talking.

"A person who makes totem poles has learned to study the animals. First, I had to study the fox. The fox is a lively creature and runs around like a small child. The fox is a symbol of a child."

He smiled and touched my hair.

"Your hair is red, like the color of the fox. You are lively and fast like the small animal the Tlingit people admire."

It was so nice to hear him say that. It made me feel warm.

"Did you paint the totem poles you carved?" I asked. "Totem poles are so big, so tall, how did you reach way up to paint them?"

Vesta's grandfather laughed.

"You paint the totems when they are lying down across the earth," he said, "before they are placed upright to stand in the sky. Long ago, we used paint brushes made from wild bushes and made all different kinds of paints from the nature around us. Some paints were made from tree bark, some from blueberries and blackberries. These old Indian paints last for hundreds of years. They never fade in the sun. Now, these paints from long ago are gone. Very few people remember them. But the totems remain."

"What do the other totem pole animals mean?" I asked. "Besides the fox totem?"

He was quiet for a moment.

"The crab is the symbol of the thief because he has so many hands. The mosquito represents teaching. When a mosquito bites, you start itching. Sometimes learning hurts."

He put the paddle down on the table next to the dinner I had brought and looked at me.

"This paddle is for you," he said. "Take it home. It will let you hear the sounds of long ago."

I felt funny. The paddle was so beautiful, but I didn't feel right taking the carving home. He picked up the paddle and handed it to me. It felt warm, warm from the heat of his hands.

"The Tlingit does not turn down any gift," he said, "but accepts it with open arms."

That is when Vesta's grandfather and I finally became friends.

Walking home that evening I buttoned my jacket right up to my chin. It was getting colder; maybe the snow would be here soon. The cool air felt good on my cheeks and through the tangles of my red hair. A very thin frost — not quite ice, not quite snow — had covered the hill behind the school yard where the totem poles stood. I walked up the hill slowly, carefully, until I reached the top. The totem poles surrounded me in a large circle and I could hear the faraway hum of water brushing the shore. A quick wind blew hard and my ears stung a little from the cold, but I didn't put up my hood. I looked straight up at the totem poles and felt the small paddle in my jacket pocket. Something was shining in my heart.

Soon Vesta and I were bringing Grandfather dinner every Thursday night. My mother taught me how to bake pink salmon with onion and lemon. Vesta taught me how to pick wild asparagus and boil it with salt. Once, Vesta and I made a blackberry pie with the berries we had picked in the fall. I learned how to chop deer meat and fry it with carrots and tiny potatoes. My mother said I would be a great chef someday. I still want to be a bush pilot.

You might think it funny that I had a grown-up like Grandfather for a friend. But he was very special, a different kind of friend who could tell you things to picture in your head, and who could make you remember how much you had to tell. Sometimes, at Grandfather's house, we would tell each other stories or carve animals out of warm, soft wood. Sometimes we would eat Tlingit candy made from dried seaweed and sugar. Sometimes we would eat too much.

One morning, after an evening at Grandfather's, Vesta did not show up at school. All day I wondered about her, looking at her empty seat. It was strange in school without her; I couldn't concentrate. I tore the corner of my composition paper without even knowing it. Then I rolled the paper into a tiny ball. Maybe she was sick. Maybe her stomach hurt from all the candy we had eaten the night before.

After all that worrying, I felt kind of silly when I saw Vesta waiting outside of school that afternoon. She didn't look like her stomach hurt, but she didn't look quite like her usual self either.

"Hey, Vesta," I called, happy to see her, "you played hooky today. Let's stay out of school together tomorrow and look on the beach for neat old boat parts."

I walked over to her and kind of hugged her left shoulder. She looked down. Maybe she was sick after all.

"Want some baseball cards?" I asked. "George Sam gave me a whole bunch of cards for that broken steering wheel we found by Mr. Teller's house."

Vesta still didn't say anything. We began walking slowly toward the docks. Just like that, without saying anything.

"Shawn," Vesta said after awhile, "my father has a new job. He has to go to a new job away from Klawock."

I can tell you, I felt really sorry for Vesta just then. My father was still in New York City. I knew how much not having your father around could hurt.

"Well, Vesta," I said, kind of hugging her again, "don't worry; you can see him holidays, and maybe in the summer, too."

Vesta shook her head.

"No, Shawn," she whispered so softly that I could hardly hear her, "my family's going with him. My whole family is going to leave Klawock."

That really took me by surprise. I stopped walking. Now I felt kind of sick.

"But you can't leave!" I said loudly. I wasn't whispering like Vesta at all. "You can't leave Klawock because you're my best friend and your house is here and we haven't decided which cave to use as our private club house!"

"I know," Vesta said. "I know."

We started walking again. The Klawock sky started to turn pink and grey like it does some afternoons. The mountains and the water and the trees looked fuzzy.

"Shawn," Vesta continued, "my family is leaving Klawock on the seaplane next week. The hunting season just hasn't been good on the island this year and my father needs other work. My mother is packing the house into boxes. She has packed my winter parka and my winter boots."

There didn't seem much else to say just then. I felt like getting angry, but knew that wouldn't help much. I felt like pretending I hadn't heard Vesta whisper, but knew she would just speak again, maybe louder next time. My whole self began to hurt like I had fallen down the hill behind my house or had been pushed hard into the mud during a game of tag.

We were at the docks by then. A small seaplane was rocking in the waves in the Klawock water. The pilot was untying the ropes to get ready for take-off. Two boys were helping him. They were laughing and talking quickly. Vesta and I watched the pilot climb into the plane and laugh with the boys. He started up the engine. The two boys stepped back on the dock and were suddenly quiet.

The plane turned slowly and the engine got louder. I could just see the pilot through the plane window. Maybe he was smiling; maybe he was waving. The plane moved faster and faster until finally it left the water. Vesta and I were very quiet. We watched the plane get smaller and smaller, like a strange crooked bird in the pink Klawock sky.

Just like that, Vesta's father had found a job in a cannery in Ketchikan. A cannery is a factory where fish are cleaned and put into cans to be sent all over the country. There are a lot of dumb canneries in Alaska because there's so much dumb fish.

What I can't stand is when things happen that are unfair and there's absolutely nothing you can do. And there wasn't anything at all I could do about Vesta's leaving. Each day at school, she got quieter and quieter. We were still friends. We still passed each other notes. We still walked down to the docks after school. But each day, something would get in the way of our talking the way we used to talk. It was almost as if Vesta had already left Klawock.

That evening before Vesta's family was to leave, I told my mother that I wasn't going to school anymore and that was that.

"Don't be silly, Shawn," she said as she looked under the sink at the water pipes. "Of course you're going to school."

"No, I'm not," I said. I might have crossed my arms right then, because crossing your arms can make you look quite serious. "I'm not going to school anymore, not ever. *Never!* No one else at school is like Vesta. No one else there is my friend."

My mother didn't say anything for a while. She wiped her hands on an old striped towel and stood up slowly. I noticed she looked tired.

"Shawn," she said, her voice real low, "there are plenty of other children at school to be your friends. You're just being silly and you know it. You're acting like a baby. Now, I want you to go into your room and start doing your homework for tomorrow."

I stood still for a moment. For some reason, I wanted to say something else to my mother, to touch her hand or maybe move closer. But I didn't move at all.

"Please, Shawn," she said, "I'm very tired and still have to finish fixing the sink before I can even start in on my school papers. I just don't have the energy to argue with you now."

Something hurt inside me when she said that. I rubbed my eyes for a minute. My face felt hot. I didn't say anything, but, pulling at my tangled hair, I walked slowly back into my room.

So I went to school the next day after all. Vesta was sitting at her desk when I came in. She was staring straight ahead. I took off my jacket and sat down in my chair. I didn't feel angry any more. I didn't feel hurt. What I felt was kind of empty, like when you don't eat for a long while, or when you've had a bad dream that kept you awake all night long. But not talking to Vesta wouldn't make that feeling go away.

I turned to her.

"You know, Vesta," I said, "maybe you'll like Ketchikan. Maybe it won't be so bad after all."

Vesta looked at me. She had a way of looking at you real hard, without even blinking.

"Shawn," Vesta said, "I'm scared. I'm scared of leaving Klawock and scared of going to Ketchikan."

I felt as though I had been running and lost my breath. Vesta never seemed scared of anything! It didn't make sense for her to be scared of anything at all.

"Vesta," I said, "don't be scared. It won't be so different in Ketchikan. You'll make all kinds of new friends there. You'll be able to walk down to the docks and watch the seaplanes land just like we do here."

"I've never lived anywhere but Klawock," she said. "I've never lived on any other island or gone to any other school. There will be a lot of people in Ketchikan, people I don't know. There will be long streets that wind and turn, a lot of tall buildings, and a lot of fast cars. What if I get lost?"

I had never heard Vesta say so much all at once. I put my hand on hers.

"Hey, Vesta," I said. "There are a lot of tall buildings and a lot of people in New York City, where I used to live. I never got lost."

Vesta smiled.

"But Shawn," she said, "you're real smart. You know how to find your way."

You can't imagine how I felt when Vesta said that. *She* was the smart one! She was the one who could catch the biggest fish, dig the deepest holes, pick the most berries.

"You'll know what to do when you get there," I said. "You'll meet a best friend in Ketchikan who will show you what to do and help you find your way. I know you will."

By that time, the rest of the kids had come into school so Vesta and I couldn't talk anymore. In fact, we really didn't have much of a chance to talk again before she left. What I remember most about her leaving was that morning talk we had in school, and how much like me Vesta, my friend from Klawock, really was.

After school, I didn't go down to the docks to see Vesta off. I was afraid I would get angry or even cry. Instead, I hugged her quickly on the school steps.

"You'll always be my friend," I said into her ear. And then I ran all the way home.

Have you ever thought that time had maybe stopped passing? I know it sounds strange, but that's what happened to me when Vesta left Klawock. I would wonder to myself, "How will this whole day pass?" I'd look at the empty desk next to mine at school and think that nothing would ever again be the same.

I know, in my head, it's better to talk things out, but when I feel scared, I don't like to talk about it. And when I feel scared without telling anyone, something strange happens. It's as if my face shrinks and my head grows a wide hat. Under that hat I think whatever I want and nobody can ever tell. Under that hat, I can stay angry all of the time.

The one person I might have felt like talking to, or maybe just being around, was Grandfather. But after Vesta left, he seemed to disappear. It might seem strange not to be able to find someone in a village as small as Klawock, but that's exactly what happened. On Thursday night, I packed a dinner of stew and wild asparagus, but when I went to Grandfather's house, there was no one there. Early in the morning, before I went to school, I rushed down to the docks where he would sometimes go fishing. Brushing the salt and the fog from my face, I walked back and forth, watching and waiting. He was nowhere to be seen. After school, before I went home, I stopped in Mr. Petrovitch's store and asked if anybody had seen Grandfather.

"That's funny," Mr. Petrovitch said, unloading a new shipment of wool hats and canned vegetables. "I haven't seen the old man in about a week. Just can't help you, Shawn."

To be honest, I thought that maybe Grandfather had decided to go with Vesta and her family to Ketchikan. That hurt. He could have at least said goodbye. He could have at least touched my arm the way he did and smile at my red hair. I could have leaned against him and maybe hugged him just a little. Maybe I could have told him how safe and special he made me feel and that he was my friend.

Then one day, right in the middle of my school lunch, I remembered. I remembered how Grandfather once told Vesta and me about the cabin right in the middle of the Klawock woods.

"It's where I lived as a boy," he had said. "It's where my memories, sweet and sad, still are alive."

He had planned to take Vesta and me to that cabin one day. We were going to stay overnight and light a fire and listen to Grandfather tell us stories of long ago.

"The cabin!" I said. George Sam, who was sitting next to me pulling off the brown crusts from his fish sandwich, looked at me like I was crazy. "I bet he's at the cabin!" And then, without telling the teacher, I left school to find Grandfather's cabin in the Klawock woods.

It really wasn't difficult because where there was once only wild woods, there was now a small road on the edge of town. Grandfather had told us how the town had slowly covered the forest like a huge blanket of houses and roads.

"The path by the garbage dump where you two saw the small bear," Grandfather had said, "was once all trees and bushes and full of wild animals. Where there is now a gravel road, that's where I lived as a boy."

The cabin, I saw, when I finally reached the small road, was so little and old that, at first, I thought I was in the wrong place. The walls sagged as if about to fall, and the steps were crooked and broken and covered with dark moss. There might have been all kinds of bugs living in a cabin like that.

I opened the door without knocking and felt a strange silence fall all around. Grandfather was there. The floor creaked softly as I walked over to him. He was kneeling in front of an old stove, rubbing his hands as if to keep warm. I saw at once that he had been waiting for me to come.

"Young Shawn," he said, motioning for me to sit by his side. "The fire is warmer now that you are here."

"I'm happy to see you, Grandfather," I said. "I thought that you had left with Vesta, left on the seaplane to live in Ketchikan. I thought you had moved to a new home in Ketchikan."

"A new home?" Grandfather touched my arm with his large, brown hand. "One is old and weak. An old man's home cannot be moved. An old man is left alone."

"But Grandfather," I said, feeling a sudden chill, "you're not weak, and you're not all that old."

Grandfather shook his head.

"A family has lived in Klawock for many years, many seasons. Now the deer have gone, now the family leaves. But the totems have been carved here and an old man cannot leave the only home he knows."

I reached out and touched Grandfather on his shoulder.

"Grandfather," I said, so softly it was almost a whisper, "you know that my father didn't move with me to Klawock. You know that he stayed in New York City. Well, I never really talk about this much, but I really miss him — a lot. Sometimes, I cry at night and can't sleep at all."

Grandfather looked up and touched my face gently, but I kept talking. I somehow couldn't seem to stop.

"And when I moved here, I hated Klawock and hated school and everything. But you and Vesta changed all that. I even wrote to my father about how you and Vesta changed that. You're my friends. My best friends. Because of you, I don't feel so alone."

No one said anything just then. I could hear the fire hiss and crackle, and could feel the cold, damp old cabin begin to get warm. Suddenly Grandfather nodded and looked up.

"Shawn," he said slowly, "an old man

has forgotten that a Tlingit lives as a man walks. He doesn't turn back. If he must leave something behind, it is left behind. He knows that what is left will return in some other form, in some other way. An old man has forgotten."

"You and I will stick together now," I said quickly. "We'll be each other's special family and we'll be each other's friend."

Grandfather took my face in both of his hands. His skin smelled of wood and smoke from a cedar fire.

"We will each look through a window," he said quietly. "Through me, you will see how Vesta lives. Through you, I will also see. We will be drawn to the side of those who give us strength, and what is left behind will stay within us."

What Grandfather said made a lot of sense. I hugged him, although I had never done that before. Grandfather laughed and hugged me back. Then we both leaned toward the fire, and together felt its warmth fill every corner of Grandfather's old house.

D

ear Vesta,

Remember that special spot by the Klawock lake, where you can hear the wolves call out to their friends? Grandfather showed me how to answer back. He said he taught you, too, a long time ago.

Things here are pretty much like always. The seaplanes still come in twice a day, and the bush pilot, Bob, still lets me unload boxes and the mail. He brought me a chocolate turkey for Thanksgiving all the way from Seattle. I shared it with the kids in my bush pilot club.

Mr. Sam brought us some seal liver, and when he left, my mother made a face and stuck the liver in the back of the refrigerator. Later, she fried it for me, and it tasted OK so I don't know what her face was for. Maybe she still has to get used to living in Klawock and eating Klawock food. But she seems a lot happier lately. She's made a few friends, too. I guess my mother and father will stay separated for awhile longer. At least until next summer. My mother says we'll see.

Here's the strange thing. I'm not so sure I want to go to New York City for Christmas. I can't wait to see my father and to see if my hamster got fatter. I can't wait to look at the New York City Christmas windows in the stores and hunt for

dimes in the phone booth across the street from my old school. But I get a funny feeling when I think of missing Christmas in Klawock. Grandfather says on Christmas all the kids go to each other's houses and get presents, like Tlingit candy and oranges stuck with cloves. I wonder what my mother will do without me to dress up in a dumb Christmas skirt and to tie up my hair with dumb ribbons. I wonder who will bring Grandfather his dinner.

Yesterday I saw the first Klawock snow. The wind was so cold, I wore long underwear to keep my skin from hurting. My mother made me a red hat with ear flaps. She says it goes with my red hair. I think so, too. My hat is nice and warm, but when the wind blows hard, on my way

home from school, I like to take it off and feel my hair flying all around my face.

I hope you are liking Ketchikan. How is your new school and your new house? Write back as soon as you can. I miss you.
Love,
                                    Shawn

P.S. In the late afternoon, the Klawock sky turns pink. If I walk up the hill behind the school yard, I can see the totem poles shining in the moving light. If I stand close to the one with the red fox on top and hold my breath, I can hear the calls of friends from long ago.